For a free color catalog describing Gareth Stevens Publishing's list of high-quality books
and multimedia programs, call 1-800-542-2595 (USA) or 1-800-461-9120 (Canada).
Gareth Stevens Publishing's Fax: (414) 225-0377.
See our catalog, too, on the World Wide Web: http://gsinc.com

Library of Congress Cataloging-in-Publication Data available upon request from publisher.
Fax: (414) 225-0377 for the attention of the Publishing Records Department.

ISBN 0-8368-1625-0 (lib. bdg.)
ISBN 0-8368-1699-4 (softcover)

First published in North America in 1996 by
**Gareth Stevens Publishing**
1555 North RiverCenter Drive, Suite 201
Milwaukee, Wisconsin  53212  USA

Text © 1994 by Michael Coleman. Illustrations © 1994 by Chris Mould.
First published in 1994 by Oxford University Press, Walton Street, Oxford OX26DP, England.

Printed in the United States of America

1 2 3 4 5 6 7 8 9 01 00 99 98 97 96

# HANK THE CLANK

## CHRIS MOULD
## &
## MICHAEL COLEMAN

Gareth Stevens Publishing
**MILWAUKEE**

ONCE upon a tomb there was a ghost named Hank. Now, Hank's job was to clank a ball and chain around an old churchyard.
This was a pretty grave place, not much fun at all in fact.

It was also very lonely which made Hank feel quite miserable because he was a naturally high spirited sort of ghost.

He longed for a few laughs, and most of all for someBODY who liked him.

The trouble was, every time he tried to make a friend the same thing happened.

For instance, early in the morning, while it was still dark, he might see a nice friendly-looking person waiting at the bus stop outside the churchyard gates.

And so he would go over to say HELLO

He would clank his way across the grass and then pop his head over the churchyard wall.

They'd never even said something like, 'Sorry, were you spooKing to me?'

All they'd ever said was,

EEKK!

..before running away as fast as they possibly could.

So one night Hank decided to visit a few other ghosts to see whether they could give him any advice on......

...how to find a friend.

He clanked his way
   to the outskirts of
town,
   to an old deserted
house with broken
windows and holes
   in its roof.

This was BONAPARTE'S house.

Bonaparte was a skeleton. 'Don't ask me how to be liked', said Bonaparte. 'The only time I've ever been liked was when a dog took a fancy to one of my bones and buried it!'
Hank began to giggle.

'It was nothing to laugh at,' said Bonaparte. 'It was my funny bone.'

14

'Anyway, we skeletons don't want people to like us.'

'Why ever not?' asked Hank.

'Because,' said Bonaparte, 'we enjoy scaring people out of their skins?'

Hank was clanking away when, suddenly, Bonaparte ran after him.

'Wait for me!' he shouted.

'I want a friend too.'

'You do?' said Hank.

'Yes I do', said Bonaparte sadly.

'And I make no bones about it.'

Hank and Bonaparte went out into the countryside to an old ruined castle. Through the big thick walls they went and down into the dungeons.

Out of the shadows stepped a man with his head tucked underneath his arm.

'My name's WARD,' he boomed. 'IT USED TO BE EDWARD, AND THEN I LOST MY ED. HAHA.'

'My name's Hank', said Hank. 'Can you tell me how to find a friend?'
'NO', boomed Edward.
'Can you lower your voice?' asked Bonaparte.

Edward put his head down on the ground. 'How's that?' Hank said that was better. Then he asked about making friends again.
'I don't need friends', said Edward. He looked up at his body, which was walking around on its own.
'I can talk to myself, see!'

Hank and Bonaparte
Went on their way. But
no sooner had they
left than
Edward came
running after them.
'Wait for me!' he shouted. 'I didn't mean it!
I want a friend as well.'
'Of course you do,' said Hank. 'We all need a
shoulder to cry on sometimes.'

They hadn't gone far when a witch whooshed down in front of them.
'Do you like my broomstick?' she cackled.
'I won it in a sweep. Ha-ha-ha-ha!!'
'Who are you?' asked Hank.
'Have you got any friends?'

'My name's Gladys,' said the witch, and I've got billions of friends.'

'Whenever I call on somebody, they always say they're Gladys me!'

'You are lucky,' said Hank. Suddenly Gladys began to cry.
'It's not true. They don't say that. They say "Buzz off".'

'Then you must come with us', said Hank.
'We're going to keep on looking until we find a friend.'
So every night Hank, Bonaparte, Edward, and Gladys
went out and about.
But it was
hopeless.

PLEASE KEEP
OFF
THE GRASS

It seemed as if
everybody was frightened of them.
Which they were, of course.

28

'Right, then,' said Hank, 'if people aren't going to be friends with us, then I say we start being really horrible to people.'

'And we'll start with...her!'
He had just seen an old lady. She was walking up the long, winding driveway of an enormous house.

Hank clanked loudly up behind her.
  Clank, Clank, went his ball and chain.
'Moaaaann', moaaaned Hank.

MMOOoAAANI

The old lady looked around.
She didn't seem frightened at all.
Hank moaned even louder. 'Moooddaann!!'
he went. 'I'm gooing to haauunt yoou!
Evverry dayy! And especially on a
                              Mooaannday.'

But still the old lady didn't seem frightened.
In fact, as she reached the door of the great house she looked quite pleased.

They couldn't understand it. They tried again.

All four of them moaned. Bou did they moannn.

Mooooo

Hank clanked,
Edward groaned,
Bonaparte
rattled,

Gladys
screeched.

They really gave
the old lady her
moenies worth.

aannnn!

But the old lady
just smiled.
'Are you really ghosts?'
she asked. 'All of you?'
'Yeeeeeeesss,'
said Hank in his
most ghostly voice.
'Yesss! Yesss! Yesss!'
said the others.

25

The old lady just smiled again. A big, beaming smile, as though she really was pleased to see them.
'Wonderful!' she cried. Because she really was pleased to see them.

'You mean...' said Hank '... you don't want to run away from us?'

'No!' said the old lady. 'In fact... how would you all like to come and live here in this house?'

Hank couldn't believe his ears. A friend, they'd found a friend!

'This is a stately home, you see,' the old lady said.
'It costs so much money to run that unless I get lots of visitors paying to look around I won't be able to keep it. But if it had four lovely ghosts like you... Well, people would come in their thousands.'

SPOOKY MANSION

'Oh, yes,' said Hank happily. 'I would like to live here.' 'And me,' said Bonaparte. 'And me,' said Edward. 'And me,' said Gladys. 'You'll be Gladys me.' 'I'm sure I will,' said the old lady. And so, from that day on that's what happened.

The old lady earned lots of money.
Edward was elected head ghost,
Bonaparte had a rattling good time,
and Gladys brushed up on her broomstick flying.
And Hank the Clank rattled his chain and really had a *ball!*